Little Else
GHOST HUNTER

To Snow Hunt
J.H

To Andrew Grant
'animal whisperer'
B.N

Little Else

GHOST HUNTER

Julie Hunt & Beth Norling

ALLEN&UNWIN

The
Lost Herd

Little Else was on the run. She was wanted for cattle duffing, horse rustling and helping known felons escape from the law. She usually kept to the cover of the hills, but her horse, Outlaw, had thrown a shoe. In the dark of night, she hid her gang of bushrangers outside the town of Witt's End.

'We can't go on until his shoe is fixed,' she whispered.

'But the police are on our heels,' said Firebolt Jim.

'They'll catch up to us by morning,' said Lightning Jack.

'Let's go on to Mt Lost,' urged Dangerous Dan. 'We can fix the shoe later.'

Little Else turned to Outlaw. 'What do you reckon?' she whispered.

Outlaw snorted. 'Don't put the cart before the horse.'

'I'm tired,' said Toothpick, who was the newest member of the gang. 'Do bushrangers always travel all night?'

'All night and all day,' said Little Else. 'I need to get Outlaw to the blacksmith. Wait here.' She leapt into the saddle. 'I'll be quick as a flash.'

Iron Bob was working late. His face glowed in the light of the forge. Sparks flew as his hammer struck the anvil.

'Ah, Little Else!' he cried. 'Still wild and free?'

'Yes,' said Little Else. 'But I'm on the run.
I'm wanted for horse theft and unarmed holdup.'

'What did you hold up?'

'The mail coach,' said Little Else.
'But only for five minutes.'

'Come in,' Iron Bob shouted. 'You're welcome
any time of the day or night. I'm making shoes
for the Witt's End Gift. It's race day tomorrow.'

'You remember Outlaw?' said Little Else,
as she led him into the workshop. Two other
horses were inside, waiting to be shod.

'How could I forget?' Iron Bob exclaimed.
'Magnificent animal! Wide chest. Big heart.
Honest as the day is long.'

'Maybe not that honest,' Outlaw
whispered to Little Else.

'Look at the size of his hoofs!'
the blacksmith cried. 'He's
monumental. You could go a
long way on a horse like that.'

'I intend to,' said Little
Else. 'We're heading
to Mt Lost.'

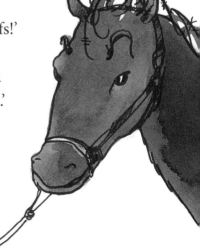

'Mt Lost!' he cried. 'Are you going in search of the Lost Herd?'

'No,' said Little Else. 'What herd?'

Iron Bob pointed to an ancient poster nailed to the wall. The paper was cracked and covered in coal smoke, but Little Else could make out the words.

LOST OR STOLEN
50 PRIZE CATTLE.
MISSING IN FLOOD WATERS
NEAR THE BROKEN RIVER.
VALUABLE BREEDING STOCK
WORTH THEIR WEIGHT IN GOLD.
REWARD INCLUDES

The bottom of the poster was torn off.

'Has anyone gone looking for them?' Little Else asked.

'Plenty. But they never came back. Those cattle were lost a hundred years ago. What can I do for you, Little Else? We'd better be quick. See that horse over there?' Iron Bob pointed with his hammer. 'He's a police horse. They'll be coming to collect him soon.'

'Outlaw has thrown a shoe and the others are loose.'

'Let me see.' Iron Bob lifted one of Outlaw's enormous hoofs.

Little Else went over to the police horse. 'What's your name?' she asked.

'Trigger, sir,' he replied.

'You don't have to call me sir,' said Little Else. 'What's it like being a police horse?'

'Tough, sir,' said Trigger. 'I'd rather be with the bushrangers.'

'Would you like to join my gang?' Little Else asked. 'We need another horse. Outlaw is carrying five of us.'

'Yes, sir!'

The other horse in the blacksmith's shop was tall and sleek.

'Are you with the police too?' Little Else asked.

The horse flinched. 'Certainly not. My name is Noble Reward. I'm the favourite for the Witt's End Gift.'

Just then a man came into the blacksmith's shop. He was small and wizened and he had a sharp eye. 'Sorry to call so late, Iron Bob,' he said. 'I've got Long Shot outside. Can you shoe him as well?'

'If you give me a tip for the race,' said Iron Bob.

'Long Shot in the first. Lady Luck in the second and you can be sure Noble Reward will win the Gift. All my horses are in top condition. Bet on any of them and you can't go wrong.'

'Thanks,' said Iron Bob. 'Bring him in.'

The little man led a horse that looked much like Noble Reward. He was fine and sleek and his coat gleamed. He pranced around the workshop.

'Oh no,' Iron Bob groaned. 'Here's trouble.'

Little Else went up to the horse and blew in his nostrils. He immediately quietened. She spoke to him softly. 'Iron Bob's a good blacksmith. He won't hurt you.'

'You're a horse whisperer!' the racehorse said. 'That's a rare gift.'

'I got it from my grandfather,' Little Else told him. 'When he whispered, horses whispered back.'

'The girl's talking to herself,' the small man remarked.

'That's Little Else,' said Iron Bob. 'Trick rider, horse whisperer and bushranger.'

Billy Sparrow

'**I'm Billy Sparrow.**
I used to be a champion jockey.
Now I'm the best trainer in the country.'
The little man stood back and studied
Little Else with his head on the side. 'You look
different from your picture in the Wanted poster.
Your hair is wilder and your outfit is worn out.'

'A bushranger's life is no picnic,' Little Else
replied, looking him in the eye. They were
exactly the same size.

'Have you ever thought of becoming a jockey?'

'No,' said Little Else. 'I'm on the run.'

There were voices outside the blacksmith's shop. Iron Bob went to the door. 'Sorry, constable,' he said. 'I haven't shod Trigger yet.'

Billy Sparrow pushed a jockey's cap into Little Else's hand. 'Quick, put this on,' he said. 'And this.' He whipped a silk shirt out of his back pocket.

Little Else jammed the cap over her head and did up the strap. She put on the shirt. Outlaw moved behind the other horses.

'Evening, Billy,' the policeman said as he walked into the workshop. 'Any tips for tomorrow?'

'Princely in the first. Best Bet the second. And who will win the Gift is anyone's guess,' said the trainer.

'Got a new apprentice, I see?'

'Yes,' said Billy. 'I'm trying him out.'

'I'll come back tomorrow,' the policeman told Iron Bob.

Little Else breathed a sigh of relief. 'Thank you,' she said.

'My pleasure.' Billy Sparrow gave a little bow. 'Could you do something for me in return?'

'What is it?' asked Little Else.

'Ride Long Shot in the first. No one will recognise you in the silks. He'll win for sure.'

'I told you, I don't want to be a jockey.'

'Listen, I'll be frank with you,' said the trainer. 'I can't get a jockey to ride him.'

'Why not?'

'He's too fast. The jockeys can't take the pace.'

'What happens to them?' asked Little Else. 'Do they fall off?'

'Fall apart is more like it,' Long Shot snorted. 'I'm the fastest horse there is.'

'Why am I asking you?' Billy Sparrow muttered. 'You're only a kid and I reckon you might be scared.'

'I'm not scared,' said Little Else. She turned to Noble Reward. 'You're a racehorse. Tell me, is he really that fast?'

'He's faster than the speed of light,' the horse replied.

Little Else's eyes shone. 'That fast?' She put her hands on her hips. 'I'll do it,' she said. 'But on one condition. You lend me three getaway horses once the race is over.'

'Done!' said Billy Sparrow. 'But you have to return them within a month. With interest.'

'What's interest?' Little Else asked.

'Something extra.'

'All right,' said Little Else. 'I'll bring you a cow from the Lost Herd.'

The trainer gasped. 'No!' he said.

'Yes!' said Little Else. 'I promise.'

'It's a deal,' said Billy Sparrow.

Mt Lost

'**She'll need provisions**,' Iron Bob told Billy. 'Food, waterbags, rope, blankets, candles.'

'What do I need the rope for?' Little Else asked.

'The cattle muster. Can you throw a lasso?'

'Of course,' said Little Else. 'I did rope tricks as part of my rough riding act at the circus.'

'And she'll need a packhorse,' said Iron Bob. 'To carry it all.'

'I'll be that,' Trigger whispered to Little Else.

'Take this horse,' Little Else said. 'Load him up.'

Billy Sparrow looked at Trigger. 'Have you got any whitewash?' he asked Iron Bob.

The blacksmith went out the back and returned with a tin and brush. Billy painted a white blaze down the middle of Trigger's face.

'That's better,' he said. 'I don't want the police to recognise him. Shoe him quickly, Iron Bob, and I'll be away.'

Iron Bob set to work.

'Of course, some people don't believe the Lost Herd exists,' he said, as he beat the metal into shape. 'Some people say the cattle drowned in the flood a hundred years ago.'

'They exist, all right,' said Billy Sparrow. 'They're out there somewhere.'

Iron Bob lifted Trigger's hoofs and nailed on one shoe after the other.

'They say once you cross the Broken River you're as good as lost.' He began making a giant shoe for Outlaw. 'You'll have to keep your wits about you, Little Else.'

'I don't even know which way to go,' she said.

'Head west to the Mt Long Gone turn-off. Go through the Back-of-Beyond until you reach the town of Havock. Cross the Broken River then climb up Windy Ridge. Go to the end of Finger Point then jump across Deadman's Gap to Desolation Bluff. From there, you'll see the Long Plains and Mt Lost. Got it?'

'No,' said Little Else.

Iron Bob took down the poster from the wall. Bits of the old paper crumbled to dust in his hands. 'There's a map on the back,' he said.

Race day

Little Else was nervous the next morning.
So was her gang.

'You're taking a big risk,' said Firebolt Jim.
'You might get caught.'

'You've never been a jockey before,' ·
said Dangerous Dan.

'You should have asked us first,'
said Lightning Jack.

'What happens if you fall apart?'
said Toothpick. 'We'll have no leader for our gang.'

'Fortune favours the bold,' said Little Else.
'Outlaw, take Toothpick and go on ahead.
We'll meet you at the turn-off to Mt Long Gone.

'Can't I stay with you?' asked Toothpick.

'No,' said Little Else. 'You're new to
bushranging and this may involve a fast getaway.'
She turned to the others.

'Firebolt Jim, Dangerous
Dan and Lightning Jack –
you wait here. Long
Shot's race is on first
so I should be back soon
with a horse for each of you.'

Firebolt suddenly leapt to his feet.
'What's that? I heard something!'
'That'll be Billy Sparrow. He's coming
with the packhorse and supplies.'
Billy pushed through the bush and appeared
in the clearing where the gang was hiding.
'All set?' he asked. 'Long Shot's already
at the racetrack.'
Billy had brought fresh silks. Yellow
with purple diamonds. He also had
a small pair of jodhpurs. Little Else
swapped her faded cowgirl skirt
with the tattered fringe.
The jodhpurs fitted perfectly.
'There!' said Billy.
'No one will pick you out
from the other jockeys.'

18

Little Else told Trigger to go with Outlaw.

'Goodbye gang!' she called.

'Good luck,' cried Toothpick. 'Keep it together.'

'Don't lose your nerve,' said Dangerous Dan.

'And tuck that hair under your cap,'
said Firebolt Jim.

They arrived at the track two minutes
before the first race was due to begin.

'No point in hanging around and letting
people recognise you,' Billy said.

Long Shot was restless. He was waiting
at the starting line.

'Do you think you can stand the pace?'
he asked, as she jumped into the saddle.

'I don't know,' she replied. 'When I was at the
circus I would fix my eyes on a point far away
to keep my balance.'

'What did you do at the circus?'

'Everything. High wire, slack rope, rough
riding, tumbling, juggling and bareback
acrobatics. My name was La Petite Elsié and
I was the best.'

'Like me,' said Long Shot. 'I'm the best.'

Little Else leaned down along his neck and twisted her hands in his mane. 'When I was learning trapeze I would throw my heart to the other side and let the rest of me catch up later.'

'You work a lot like I do,' said Long Shot.

'I'm going to fix my eyes on the finishing post and hold on for grim death.'

'I don't want you to die,' said Long Shot. 'But you might.'

The starting gun fired and Long Shot shot
forward like a bullet. Little Else's feet flew
out of the stirrups and her legs streamed
out behind her. The wind roared in her ears.
Her eyes watered. She tried to focus on the
winning post, but the speed they were
travelling at blew the thought of it out
of her head. Everything was a blur.

Little Else realised she had made a terrible mistake. She was losing her grip. No one could stand this speed. Not even Jason the Human Javelin who worked at the circus.

'Oh help!' she cried as the cap on her head fell apart and her hair streaked out. She closed her eyes and screamed, 'Grandma!'

Grandma! That was a thought she could hold. She pictured her grandmother sitting in front of their hut at Stony Gully.

'Keep your eye on the prize,' Grandma said calmly. Little Else opened her eyes and fixed her gaze on the winning post. 'Keep your head,' Grandma said. 'Don't forget to breathe.'

Long Shot's the

Little Else took a deep breath. The winning post was just up ahead. She only had to hold on for three more seconds. Two more seconds…
One second…

'And it's Long Shot by two hundred lengths!' came the race-caller's voice through the loud hailer. 'Ladies and gentlemen, the race is over before it has begun. Long Shot has come in at a hundred to one!'

It took Long Shot three circuits of the track
to slow down to a normal horse's gallop.
Then he jumped the rails and left the track.
Two other horses threw their jockeys and
followed with their reins dangling.
One of them was Noble Reward.

'I'm not staying to win the Witt's End Gift,'
he said, as he galloped alongside Little Else.
'I'm through with racing. I've never liked it.
Not after what happened to Fast Light.'

'Who's Fast Light?' Little Else asked.

'My sister. She went blind in one eye
and they sent her to the knackers.'

'I know her!' cried Little Else.
'She's not at the knackers now!'

There was no time to explain.
They raced out of Witt's End and met the others
at the Mt Long Gone turn-off. Then they all
took the road to Havock.

'My name is Lady Luck,' said the third horse.
'What's the plan?'

'Long story short – we're going to cross
the Broken River and find the Lost Herd,'
said Little Else.

Wild & free

L ittle Else and her gang travelled for days
through the Back-of-Beyond. Lightning
Jack rode Noble Reward. Firebolt Jim rode
Long Shot, after the horse promised Little Else
he would not break out of a trot.
Dangerous Dan was on Lady Luck.

'Tell her I'm not really dangerous,'
he said to Little Else. 'It's just a name
I use to keep myself brave.'

'Tell him I'm not really lucky,' said Lady Luck.

The two children rode Outlaw. Little Else
sat in front and Toothpick sat behind.
Trigger carried the gear.

'This is fun,' said Toothpick.
'I love this Wild Roaming life.'

'Whoa up!' yelled Little Else.
'Time to set up camp.'

Lightning Jack made a fire. Firebolt unpacked
the saddlebags. He found oats for the horses
and bread and potatoes for the gang. When
everyone had been fed, Little Else strung
a rope between two trees.

'Now the training will begin,' she said. She
found a long stick to use as a balancing pole
and handed it to Toothpick.

'Step on the rope,' she told him.
'Keep your balance.'

Toothpick did as he was told.
The rope was low. He could easily step off it.

'Make it higher,' he said.

'No. You've got to start
at the bottom and
work your way up.'

The gang watched as Toothpick took his first uncertain steps along the rope. He got halfway across then he wobbled and fell off.

'That's good,' said Little Else. 'You've got talent. Give him a round of applause.'

The gang cheered. It was nice to have some entertainment after dinner.

'Now do it again,' said Little Else.

'How about some music?'
Lightning Jack suggested.

Firebolt Jim burst into song:
'*A bushranger's life is wild and free
Little Else's gang is the gang for me...*'

Dangerous Dan sang a harmony and
Lightning Jim drummed out a beat on
the back of the frying pan.

Toothpick put one foot in front of the other in
time with the music and made it three quarters
of the way across before he had to hop down.

'Keep your centre of gravity low,' said Little
Else. 'Bend your knees and look at a spot on
the tree ahead.'

Toothpick practised until dark, then
they all went to sleep with
bushranger music
ringing in their
ears.

They woke the next morning in high spirits.
The Broken River was only a day's ride ahead
of them and the police were far behind.

Little Else took out the map and carefully
unfolded it. Bits crumbled in her hands.
The Broken River was a jagged line stretching
from the top right hand corner. Havock was
a dot alongside it.

'There's Windy Ridge,' said Firebolt. 'Look
at the wind lines. We'll have to tie on our hats.

'There's Finger Point.' Dangerous Dan pointed
to a narrow neck of land poking over a canyon.

'It looks like a bridge,' said Toothpick.
'Except it doesn't reach the other side.'

Deadman's Gap was marked with a cross.
Little Else studied the map. 'Where's
Desolation Bluff? I'm sure Iron Bob
mentioned it.'

Lightning Jack looked over her
shoulder. 'The Bluff must be on
the other side of the Gap,' he said.

'I can't see the Long Plains.
And Mt Lost is missing as well,'
said Little Else.

29

The-horse-with-one-eye

The next day they reached the tiny town of Havock. It stood on the banks of the Broken River and had one street with a post office and two huts. There was nobody about except an old white mare.

'This is a two-horse town,' she said. 'We don't get many people passing through here. If you've got any letters, this is your last chance to post them.'

'Where's the other horse?' Little Else asked.

The mare looked over the dry river bed. 'Gone,' she said wistfully. 'Gone over to the other side.'

'Have you heard of the Lost Herd?' Outlaw asked.

'Of course,' said the mare. 'They are out there somewhere.' She gazed across the dry river with a faraway look in her eye.

'Do you know anything about them?' Little Else asked.

'A man called Johnny Lost was in charge of the cattle when the floods came through. They say he was a shifty type. I reckon he stole them. But he'd be long gone by now.'

Little Else thanked the mare then she led her gang towards the Broken River. The country was the same on the other side – tall trees, low scrub and stony ground – but once they were across everything felt different.

'Look,' said Firebolt Jim. 'Hoofprints!'

They followed the hoofprints along the river bank. There was no sound, not even the wind in the trees.

'Where are the birds?' Dangerous Dan asked.

Outlaw showed the whites of his eyes.
'This country spooks me,' he said.

'I'm not feeling well,' said Dangerous Dan.
'I'm scared.'

'Look up there!' Firebolt pointed to the top
of a dead tree. An old cart was caught high in
the branches.

'No one could have crossed the river when
the flood waters were that high,' Little Else said.
'It must have been a raging torrent.
I wonder if Johnny Lost
could swim.'

The hoofprints led them to the top of a hill, then the track forked. A lot of prints went one way and only one set went the other.

'What do you reckon?' Outlaw asked.

'I say we take the road less travelled,' said Little Else.

They had not gone far when Noble Reward pricked his ears. His nostrils quivered. He pawed the ground.

'Steady,' Lightning Jack said, and stroked his neck.

'What is it?' Little Else asked the racehorse.

'It's Fast Light!' Noble Reward replied. Then he bolted along the track.

The others followed. The track opened onto a bare patch of ground where a grey horse with one blind eye stood waiting for them.

'Noble Reward, I knew you would come.'

'Fast Light, my sister!'

'I don't use my racing name anymore,' said the mare. 'Just call me the-horse-with-one-eye. Hello, Little Else.'

'How do you know each other?'
Noble Reward asked.

'In my horse-rustling days I stole some
horses from the knackers and this mare
was one of them.'

'Not stole,' said the-horse-with-one-eye.
'Rescued.'

'That's right,' said Little Else.
'How are the others?'

'All safe. They took the track that forked to
the left. It leads to a valley where the pasture
is always knee-deep and apple trees grow
wild. This way leads on to Windy Ridge and
Deadman's Gap.'

'Let's go back,' said Outlaw. 'We're obviously
on the wrong track.'

'No,' said Little Else. 'We've got to find the Lost
Herd. I made a bargain with Billy Sparrow and
I intend to keep it.'

'Will you travel with us?' she asked
the horse-with-one-eye.

'Yes,' said the mare.
'I will help you in any way I can.'

They camped that night under a new moon. Little Else strung the rope between two trees and pulled it tight. Firebolt Jim sang:

'*A bushranger's life has danger and dare*
We're going somewhere
but we don't know where.'

Toothpick climbed onto the rope.
It was higher this time.

'See those little stones on the ground?' Little Else asked. 'Pretend they are giant boulders and you're high above them.'

'That makes me dizzy,' said Toothpick.

'Good,' said Little Else. 'Get used to it.'

Toothpick slowly got his balance. Soon he was walking back and forth across the rope.

'He's going to be good,'
said the horse-with-one-eye.

'Yes,' said little Else. 'Toothpick,
bend your knees. Keep your head held high.'

She began to bounce the rope. 'Pretend it's the wind,' she said.

Toothpick had to try several times before he could keep his balance on the moving rope.

'Excellent.' said Little Else. 'Soon you'll be a real performer.'

'His name will be BirdBoy,' said the horse-with-one-eye. 'He'll fly like an eagle.'

'How do you know?' Little Else asked.

'I see it with my blind eye,' said the mare. 'Since I crossed the Broken River I see all sorts of things.'

'Do you see the Lost Herd?'

'Maybe,' said the horse-with-one-eye. 'Are they in the future?'

'I hope so,' said Little Else.

Deadman's Gap

When the gang reached Windy Ridge they had to lean forward and clasp their hands under their horses' necks to stop themselves being blown away.

The horses plodded on with their ears back and their heads down. Outlaw was in a bad mood.

'This is no fun,' he said. 'We should have gone the other way. We'll get lost out here.'

'You sound like a show pony,' said Little Else. 'I thought you liked it when the going got tough.'

'I wish I was back with Harry Blast,' Outlaw continued. 'It was all shoot-ups and hold-ups with Harry. It was good clean bushranging. I knew where I was with him.'

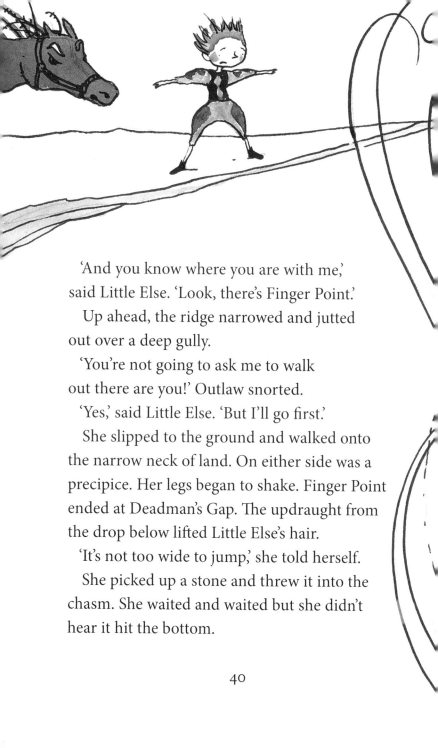

'And you know where you are with me,'
said Little Else. 'Look, there's Finger Point.'

Up ahead, the ridge narrowed and jutted
out over a deep gully.

'You're not going to ask me to walk
out there are you!' Outlaw snorted.

'Yes,' said Little Else. 'But I'll go first.'

She slipped to the ground and walked onto
the narrow neck of land. On either side was a
precipice. Her legs began to shake. Finger Point
ended at Deadman's Gap. The updraught from
the drop below lifted Little Else's hair.

'It's not too wide to jump,' she told herself.

She picked up a stone and threw it into the
chasm. She waited and waited but she didn't
hear it hit the bottom.

The gang hung back.

'I don't believe the Lost Herd exists,' said Dangerous Dan. 'It's just a story. If any cattle did manage to swim across the river they would be dead by now.'

'Maybe,' said Firebolt Jim. 'But what if they had calves and the calves grew up and had more calves? What if they bred up over the years and the fifty cattle became five hundred?'

'You're dreaming,' said Lightning Jack. 'There's nothing out there. We should turn around.'

Little Else led her gang back the way they had come. She had to find another way around Deadman's Gap. But the bush soon became confusing.

Firebolt called from the rear of the party.

'What's wrong, Little Else? Just follow our hoofprints.'

'It's strange,' she said. 'We don't seem to have left any.'

All day she led them in circles.
By late afternoon they found themselves
back at Finger Point.

'Let's bite the bullet and jump the gap,'
said Little Else.

BirdBoy

Little Else never went anywhere without postcards, paper and a pencil.

Dear Gran,

I am about to cross Deadman's Gap. It's not very wide, just a long step really. But there are no second chances if you lose your footing.

I miss you and I miss Stony Gully.

Your loving grand-daughter,

Little Else X$_x$X x X$_x$X

PS I rode the fastest horse in the world. I will tell you about it ~~when~~ I come home.
          if

She put the letter under a rock, then she walked out to the end of Finger Point. The blood was thumping in her ears. *Keep your eye on the prize,* she told herself. Her knees were trembling. She thought of her early work on the trapeze and, taking a deep breath, she threw her heart across the gap. The rest of her followed easily. She looked back, amazed.

'It's simple,' she called. 'Come on. One at a time. Horses first. Take it slowly.'

The racehorses were quivering with fright but one by one they walked along the narrow neck of land and jumped the gap.

'Next!' cried Little Else, after each one. Her voice echoed around the cliffs.

Trigger jumped across.

'I'll go last,' muttered Outlaw. 'After the gang.'

Dangerous Dan and Lightning Jack went across together, holding hands.

'It's not as hard as it looks,' they said. 'I don't know why it's called Deadman's Gap.'

'Next!' cried Little Else.

'Excuse me, sir,' said Trigger. 'It's not a good idea to shout so loud. It could cause a rockfall.'

'Next!'

Firebolt Jim held his breath and leapt across.

'Next!' yelled Little Else. 'Outlaw, that's you!'

Her voice echoed around the cliffs, getting louder and louder. Outlaw trembled. The ground started to shake. Pieces of rock began splitting off Finger Point and falling into the depths below. Deadman's Gap was getting wider.

'Quick, Outlaw,' Little Else cried. 'Jump!'

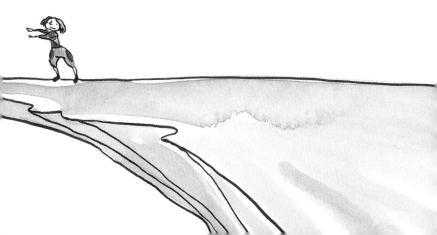

Outlaw was a big heavy horse. He thundered across the gap and landed safely on the other side just as a huge chunk of the point collapsed into the gorge. An enormous cloud of dust rose up.

'Seven, eight, nine… Someone's missing,' Little Else cried. 'Where's Toothpick?'

When the dust settled they saw Toothpick stranded on the other side. He looked very small and forlorn.'Leave me,' he called.

Just leave me

'No,' said Little Else. 'I'm not leaving anyone.
Catch this.'

She threw the rope across. Toothpick tied it to
a tree. Little Else and the gang held the other end.

'Remember everything I told you,' she said. 'Fix
your eyes on one of the diamonds on my shirt
and don't look down. I'm going to tell you a story.'

Toothpick took a step out onto the rope.

'I can't look,' said Lightning Jack.

'Me neither,' said Firebolt Jim.
'He was a lovely kid and he
had the makings of a good
bushranger.'

'The poor little mite's only had two lessons,' said Dangerous Dan.

'This is the third,' said Little Else. 'Don't let go. Listen to me…

'There was once a boy who was captured by eagles. He was a small boy. He had hollow bones and he was light as a feather. The mother eagle picked him up and took him home to her stick-nest high on a cliff face.'

'Eyrie, sir,' said Trigger. 'That nest is called an eyrie.'

Toothpick took three or four steps out over Deadman's Gap.

'"Here's dinner," the mother eagle said, as she dropped the boy into the nest. The little bald eagle chicks had only just hatched. They were covered in egg muck and their eyes weren't properly open.

'"We don't want boy," they cried. "We want mouse or rabbit."

'The big eagle flew off. While she was away, the chicks made friends with the boy.'

Little Else paused. Toothpick was halfway across the rope. His eyes were full of sky.

'Keep talking,' he said.

'Well, the chicks ate rabbit that night and the boy did too. "You'll grow fluff," they told him. "Then feathers. Then one day we'll all get chucked out of the nest together and we'll feel the wind under our wings."

'"Will we?" asked the boy.

'"Of course," said the chicks.

Toothpick was two-thirds of the way across the gap. The rope trembled.

'Don't stop,' he said.

'After dinner the boy crept to the edge of the nest and peered over. He saw tiny lights far below and above him a night sky full of stars.

'"What am I to do?" he asked the night.

'A dark wind roared up the cliff face and lifted his hair. Then it swirled into the nest and lifted sticks and rabbit gut and placed them in his lap. The boy began twisting the rabbit gut into a rope. He picked up the strongest stick and made the first rung of a very long ladder.'

Toothpick stepped off the trembling rope onto solid ground. The gang cheered.

'Did the boy get down?' Toothpick asked.

'No,' said Little Else. 'The more sticks he used for the rungs of the ladder, the smaller the nest became. This annoyed the mother eagle.'

'What happened?' asked Firebolt Jim.

'Lots,' said Little Else. 'But I haven't got time to tell you. Let's get to the other side of Desolation Bluff before dark.'

100 days

Desolation Bluff was a wild and lonely place with a view across the Long Plains. As the sun went down, the shadow of Mt Lost stretched towards them. They set up camp in the dark.

'Everyone straight to bed!' said Little Else. 'We'll leave at the crack of dawn and reach Mt Lost by lunchtime.'

The bushrangers were slow to rise the next morning.

'I don't like the way we're not leaving tracks,' said Firebolt. 'How are we to find the Lost Herd if we can't find hoofprints?'

'If the Lost Herd even exists,' said Dangerous Dan.

Toothpick was the only one who was cheerful.

He was full of his spectacular death-defying
walk across Deadman's Gap.

'Last night I dreamed I was swinging on a
trapeze made of rabbit gut and sticks,' he said.

'Sounds like Ma Calico's Bush Circus,'
said Little Else. 'Where I used to work.'

Lightning Jack made tea and porridge,
then they set off for Mt Lost. They travelled
all morning but Mt Lost did not get any closer.

'I see something up ahead,'
said the-horse-with-one-eye.

Little Else couldn't see anything
except waving grass on the Long Plains.

'What is it?'

'Mist,' said the mare. 'Fog. I can see
a shape but it keeps changing.'

Little Else checked the map and realised they
were on the bit that had fallen away in Iron Bob's
hands. When she looked back the way they had
come she couldn't see Desolation Bluff.

'I don't like this country,' said Lightning Jack.
'I say we turn back before it's too late.'

'But our journey has only just begun,'
Little Else said. 'We've got to find the Lost Herd.'

Little Else and her gang travelled for days across
the Long Plains. And days turned to weeks.

'The saddlebags are getting lighter, sir,'
said Trigger.

'Shhh,' said Little Else. She was studying the map. 'I'm trying to work out where we are.'

'We're on the part of the map that isn't there,' said Lightning Jack.

'Cheer us up, Firebolt,' said Little Else. 'Give us a song.'

Firebolt sang:
'*A hundred days to the last full moon*
We're heading for the Lost Lagoon.'

'What's the Lost Lagoon?' Little Else asked.

'Wouldn't have a clue,' said Firebolt. 'It just came into my head.'

'Well a hundred days doesn't sound very cheerful,' said Little Else.

The Lost Lagoon

It took Little Else and her gang a long time to reach the bottom of Mt Lost and an even longer time to reach the top.

'Nearly there,' she said, as they climbed the mountain.

'Nearly where?' Dangerous Dan moaned. 'We're completely lost, so lost that even if we found the Lost Herd we wouldn't be able to bring them back.'

The view from the top of Mt Lost was breathtaking. Grassy plains stretched away forever.

Suddenly the horses propped and snorted.

'Something's happening down there,' said Lady Luck.

Little Else squinted into the distance. Far, far away the ground appeared to be moving. Firebolt Jim rubbed his eyes.

'We're so tired,' he said, 'we're seeing things.'

'No, we're not!' said Little Else. 'It's the Lost Herd!'

It was true. There were thousands and thousands of cattle as far as the eye could see. They were circling a stretch of water.

'That must be the Lost Lagoon,' said Firebolt. 'We've made it!'

'Let's get down there,' said Lightning Jack.

They struggled down the other side of Mt Lost.

'Don't scare them,' said Little Else.

There was no chance of that. The cattle took no notice of the gang or the horses.

They were staring with wild eyes into the misty waters of the lagoon as if their life depended on it. They were so thin their hip bones stood out.

Little Else saw a pile of rocks near the edge of the water. She pushed her way through the cattle and began pulling it apart to see what was underneath.

'Be careful. It might be a grave.' Dangerous Dan took off his hat, but there was nothing under the stones except some old clothes and a message written on the back of a poster with a burnt stick. Some of the words were too smudged to read.

WARNING
BEWARE OF J . . . LOST. THE LAGOON
IS . . . . . . IT . . . DEAD . . .
UNDER . . . CURSE. GO BACK . . TOO
LATE. LAST WORD . GOODBYE.

Little Else turned over the paper.

LOST OR STOLEN
50 PRIZE CATTLE. MISSING IN FLOOD WATERS
NEAR THE BROKEN RIVER. VALUABLE BREEDING
STOCK WORTH THEIR WEIGHT IN GOLD.

'Poor wretch,' said Lightning Jack in a shaky voice. 'He tried and failed.'

Little Else read the bottom of the poster.

REWARD INCLUDES
A FREE PARDON AND FIFTY ACRES OF LAND.

'That was the reward for fifty cows,' she said. 'We've got five thousand! That's enough reward for all of us!'

'They don't look like they would be easy to move,' said Firebolt Jim.

The cattle were staring into the lagoon as if in a trance.

'They look like there's a spell on them,' said Toothpick.

'Or a curse,' said Lightning Jack.

'I wish I'd never come here,' said Dangerous Dan. 'I'd rather be back on the chain gang.'

'Excuse me, sir,' said Trigger. 'The saddlebags are empty.'

Little Else sat down next to the pile of rocks.

'I'm sorry, gang,' she said. 'We've run out of food. We're done for.'

A tear rolled down her face and dripped off her chin onto the poster.

'I think I'll write a letter,' said Firebolt. 'You still got that pencil?'

Firebolt Jim hadn't put pencil to paper for years, not since he forged Lady Muck's signature on a cheque he presented to the Three-Wells Trading Company.

DEAR HARRY BLAST,

It's a long time since we had that fight. I just want to tell you I caught the bullet in my teeth and spat it out. No harm was done. Let's be friends again. I still have fond memories of that time we blasted the Boomtown Bank.

Yours truly, Firebolt.

Dangerous Dan wrote to his mum.

Dear Mum,

I don't think I'm coming home so I had better say goodbye,

love,

Daniel.

'Are you going to write one, Toothpick?'
he asked.

'Can't write,' said Toothpick.

'I could have taught you,' Little Else sighed.
'But it's too late now.'

'How about I tell you what I want to say
and you write it down?' Toothpick suggested.

Little Else took the pencil. 'Go ahead.'

Dear Ma Calico,

I would like to apply for a job in your circus.
I have experience.
I walked a rope across Deadman's Gap at night
in a high wind. The rope was frayed.

Near enough, thought Little Else.
What does it matter now?

My teacher, Little Else, says
I have good balance
and am very brave.

Yours truly,

Toothpick Reed.

The poor kid, Little Else thought. She picked
up a stone and threw it into the lagoon.
'It's all my fault,' she said.
   'Yes, sir,' said Trigger.

Little Else watched the stone sink beneath the
surface of the water. A mist began to swirl.
She stared, mesmerised.
   'Aren't you going to do something, sir?'
said Trigger. 'You're the leader of the gang.'
   'What can I do?' asked Little Else. 'I'm just a kid.'
   'You'll think of something.'

The gang
went to bed
without dinner.
Little Else lay in her
blanket and looked
up at the sky. *I'll never
see Grandma again*, she thought.
She got out of bed and went to the
horse-with-one-eye.

'What do you see?' she asked her.

'Mist,' said the horse.

'And a moving light.'

'Is it Johnny Lost?'

The mare trembled. 'I don't know.
It's fading. Now I see an old lady writing a letter.'

'Grandma!'

'She's wearing an apron and hobnail boots.'

'That's her!' said Little Else.

'What does the letter say?'

'Do you think I can read?' said the mare.
'Hold on, she's saying it aloud…'

'She always does that,' said Little Else.
'When she's finished, she reads it aloud
to make sure it sounds right.'

'Shhh.' The mare pricked her ears, listening.

'Dear Little Else,' said the mare. 'Last night
I dreamed you were lost and wandering and in
terrible danger. I trust you will do the best thing
and the bravest thing and come back to me soon.

Your loving Grandmother.'

Little Else was quiet for a long time, then she
whispered into the mare's ear. 'I'm going to find
Johnny Lost.'

'No!' said the horse.

'Yes!' said Little Else. 'I'm going to find him
and I'm going to face him!'

Johnny Lost

Little **Else knew** where to look. She took off her boots and walked into the lagoon up to her ankles. It was freezing.

'I've been waiting for you,' came a wispy voice. 'I'm going to take you to the bottom of the Lost Lagoon.'

Little Else felt a movement in the water, then she saw him. His face was made of mist. His eyes were two holes and his heart was a ball of swamp gas. He hovered over the water. She was scared to death.

'Johnny Lost,' she said. 'I have something to tell you.'

Little Else had no idea what she would tell Johnny Lost. She could feel his cold breath on her neck. She thought of her grandmother and that made her feel a bit warmer.

Grandma always told her a story when she was frightened.

'There was once a man called Johnny Lost,' she began.

Johnny Lost's light flickered and came closer. Little Else backed away.

'He was in charge of fifty head of cattle. They were so valuable each one was worth its weight in gold.'

'That's me!' whispered Johnny Lost. 'You're telling my story.'

Little Else walked backwards out of the water. She bent down to put on her boots but she kept talking. 'That winter it rained and rained. The river broke its banks and the flood waters became a raging torrent.'

She talked slowly and quietly as she kept walking away from the lagoon. Johnny Lost followed. The herd parted to let them pass.

'Speak up,' he said. 'I can hardly hear.'

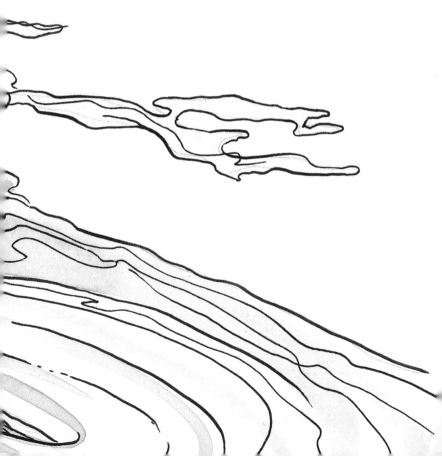

'The cattle stood on the edge of the river.' Little Else kept her voice low. She noticed that Johnny Lost's light was a little bit dimmer.

It must be because he's away from the lagoon, she told herself.

'Johnny Lost thought he would swim the cattle across,' Little Else continued. 'When they reached the other side he'd take them to a place where no one knew him and he would sell them for a fortune.'

'This is a good story,' Johnny Lost sighed. His face was changing shape. It was fraying at the edges.

'Well, Johnny Lost drove the cattle into the wild river. Some were washed away but many made it across. Then he plunged in himself. The waters swirled…'

Little Else realised she had walked right through the herd and they were a long way from the lagoon.

It was almost dawn. She could see light in the east.

'What happened?' Johnny Lost's breath was a whisper.

'The current took him. He was swept into the river and he realised he could never come back.' Little Else was guessing, but it sounded right.

'Why?' gasped Johnny Lost. 'Because they would lock him up?'

A cow bellowed. Another one answered. Soon, the whole herd was bellowing. Little Else had to shout above the noise.

'No,' she yelled. 'Because he was DEAD! He couldn't swim and he drowned crossing the Broken River.'

'Ahhh!' Johnny Lost's face glowed savagely for a second.

'He didn't know he was dead,' Little Else shouted. 'He thought he was just lost. And everything around him became lost too – the lagoon, the cattle, the people. But when Little Else found him it was a different story.'

She paused. Johnny Lost's light was a faint glimmer. They were far from the lagoon. He was losing his power.

Little Else made up a song on the spot.

'Johnny Lost, you're dead and gone
Now Little Else has spoken.
Your face dissolves.
Your light goes out.
The long lost curse is broken!'

Little Else blinked as the sun came up over the Lost Lagoon. The water looked different. It was clear. She hurried back to the gang.

'What's going on?' they cried. 'The cattle are restless. They look like they're going to rush.'

'Johnny Lost is gone. There's nothing holding them here now.'

'If they stampede we're in trouble,' said Firebolt Jim. 'We'll be trampled.'

Just then, a bullock came out of the herd. He looked different from the others.

'Edward Longhorn!' cried Little Else.

'We've met before,' she explained to the gang. 'A long time ago in my cattle-rustling days.'

The bullock walked up to Little Else and looked into her eyes. Then he lowered his head and moved among the herd, lowing softly. When he began walking towards the east, the herd followed.

'That bullock knows another way around Deadman's Gap,' said the horse-with-one-eye. 'I see five thousand cows coming up the main street of Witt's End.'

'We're on the home run now,' said Little Else. 'Who's with the herd?'

'Firebolt Jim, Lightning Jack and Dangerous Dan,' said the horse.

'I'd like to be a farmer,' said Firebolt Jim.

'So would I,' said Lightning Jack. 'I could do a lot with fifty acres.'

'What else do you see?' Little Else asked the horse-with-one-eye.

'I see horses coming over a hill above a stony gully.'

'That's my place!'

'And there's that lady...'

'Grandma!' cried Little Else. 'Can you see me standing on Toothpick's shoulders as Outlaw gallops down the hill?'

'Yes,' said the mare. 'You're going flat out. Then Outlaw stops at the very last moment...'

'Just in time for me to fit in a triple-forward flying somersault,' said Little Else, 'before I land in Grandma's arms!'